DR. DRABBLE'S
SPECTACULAR
SHRINKER-ENLARGER

DR. DRABBLE, GENIUS INVENTOR

Dr. Drabble's Remarkable Underwater Breathing Pills
Dr. Drabble's Spectacular Shrinker-Enlarger
Dr. Drabble and the Dynamic Duplicator

ISBN: 0-8499-3661-6

Printed in the United States of America
94 95 96 97 98 99 LBM 9 8 7 6 5 4 3 2 1

DR. DRABBLE'S SPECTACULAR SHRINKER-ENLARGER

Written by
Sigmund Brouwer and Wayne Davidson
Illustrated by
Bill Bell

WORD PUBLISHING
Dallas·London·Vancouver·Melbourne

P. J. and Chelsea, along with their pet skunk Wesley, walked to the marketplace with Dr. Drabble. The genius inventor had taken them to Brazil in his Flying Ship.

"Aren't the people in Brazil strange?" Chelsea said.

"Yes," P. J. agreed. "They dress and talk funny."

Dr. Drabble frowned at the kids, but didn't say anything.

The strangest thing the kids saw at the marketplace was the twin brothers behind a coffee-bean stand.

"We sell rare coffee beans," they called. "Buy from us."

The twins' noses were so large that Chelsea began to giggle loudly. "P. J.," she whispered, "look at those two men!"

P. J. giggled, too. "It looks like they have bananas for noses."

Chelsea thought that was so funny, she fell to the ground laughing.

One of the twin brothers helped her stand again. "Are you all right?" he asked.

Chelsea stared right at his nose again. She and P. J. laughed even harder.

Dr. Drabble was disappointed with them for being mean. So he thought of a plan to teach them a lesson.

"Let's go back to my laboratory on the Flying Ship," Dr. Drabble said. "I have something you should see."

On the Flying Ship, Dr. Drabble showed P. J. and Chelsea his new invention. "Tah-dah! My Spectacular Shrinker-Enlarger."

Chelsea clapped her hands. "Oh, P. J., look, Dr. Drabble's machine made all those things bigger!"

Just then, Arnie Clodbuckle came into the laboratory, holding a large watermelon. Arnie was Dr. Drabble's assistant.

Dr. Drabble aimed the Spectacular Shrinker-Enlarger at the watermelon in Arnie's arms. "Hold still, Arnie, I'll try to make the watermelon shrink," he said.

Dr. Drabble fiddled with switches on the Spectacular Shrinker-Enlarger.

ZAAAAAP! He shot a ray toward Arnie.

When Arnie looked, the watermelon was very tiny in his hands.

"The watermelon shrank!" he shouted with glee.

"Oh, dear," Dr. Drabble said. "I hit the wrong button."

Arnie realized that Dr. Drabble had enlarged him instead of shrinking the watermelon.

"Don't worry," Dr. Drabble said. "I can easily make you smaller."

ZAAAAP! Another ray hit Arnie.

Before Chelsea and P. J. could blink, Arnie was tiny. "Help!" he cried. "I don't know if Wesley wants me to be his friend or his lunch!"

Dr. Drabble sighed. "It's okay, Arnie," he said. "I just shrank you too much that time. Hold still and let me try again."

ZAAAP, Dr. Drabble hit another button on the Spectacular Shrinker-Enlarger and Arnie zoomed up to his normal size.

Dr. Drabble was now ready for his plan. "Let me try my new invention on you," he said to P. J. and Chelsea.

"Sure," they said. "That sounds like fun!"

ZAAAAP! ZAAAAP!

P. J. saw that Chelsea had ears like an elephant. Chelsea saw that P. J.'s hands and feet were as big as Frisbees.

They began to laugh at each other.

But with big ears, sounds were too loud for Chelsea. P. J. knocked things over with his big hands.

They stopped laughing.

"Fix us," they begged. "You made us look too strange!"

Dr. Drabble hit another switch on the Spectacular Shrinker-Enlarger.

Nothing happened.

"Oh, dear," he muttered. "It seems to be out of power."

"What!" Chelsea cried. "You can't leave me with big ears forever!"

"I'm afraid so," Dr. Drabble said. "Unless you get more fuel for the Spectacular Shrinker-Enlarger."

"What kind of fuel?" P. J. asked.

"Funny you should ask," Dr. Drabble said. (His plan was working perfectly.)

"Remember the twin brothers with the big noses? The Spectacular Shrinker-Enlarger needs more of their rare coffee beans."

"Can you send Arnie to get them?" Chelsea asked.

"He will be busy all day," Dr. Drabble said. "You two will have to go."

"But we can't," P. J. moaned. "Everyone will laugh at us."

"We'd rather stay in our room," Chelsea said.

And they did.

They soon discovered that big ears and big hands made life difficult.

Chelsea could hear so well, even a whisper sounded like a loud scream.

P. J. tripped every time he tried to walk. His socks didn't fit, either.

Finally, P. J. and Chelsea decided to go to the marketplace to get the coffee beans.

It was hard for them to run. P. J.'s feet were clumsy. Chelsea had to be careful that her ears did not catch on anything.

Every person who saw them laughed out loud. Little children pointed and stared.

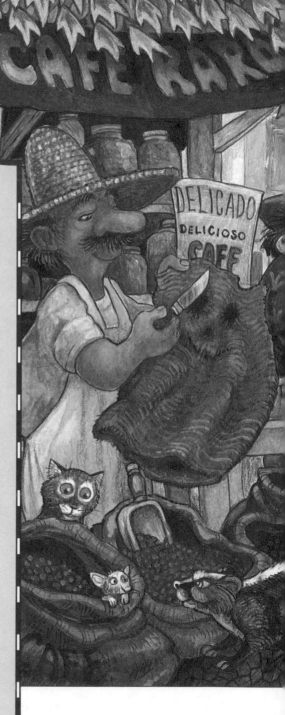

P. J. and Chelsea finally reached the rare coffee-bean stand.

"May we please have some beans?" Chelsea asked the twins. "We are sorry for laughing at you today."

"Yes," P. J. added, "if you laugh at us now, we will understand."

"Oh, no," the first one said. "We know how bad it feels to be laughed at."

"Yes," the second one said, "even though we look different, we don't feel different from anyone else."

"You may have as many beans as you need," they said kindly. "In fact, we'll even make burlap sacks to cover you so that people won't laugh anymore."

The kind twins walked with the children back to Dr. Drabble's Flying Ship.

Dr. Drabble was waiting for them. "I see you finally decided to get the beans," he said. "I hope you learned something."

"We did," P. J. said.

"Good," Dr. Drabble nodded. "You see, I really didn't need those beans. I just wanted you to know that the way people look on the outside doesn't mean anything about the way they are inside."

"We also learned how much it hurts when people laugh at you," Chelsea added.

Dr. Drabble smiled.

ZAAAAP! ZAAAAP!

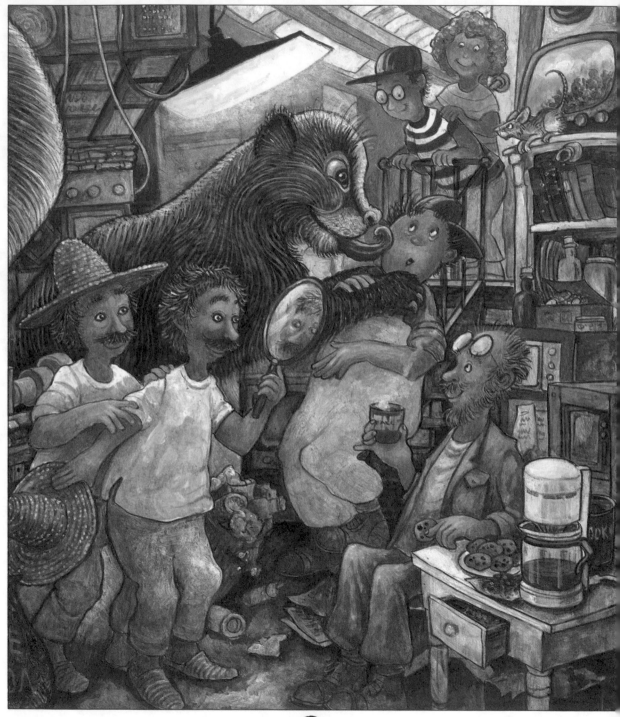